For Gene, Sean, Steph, and Leah
Inspired by "Foxalito," a poem by Gene Berson
J. L.

For my Lisa Jane
D. M.

First edition 2018

Library of Congress Catalog Card Number pending
ISBN 978-0-7636-8814-1

18 19 20 21 22 23 LEO 10 9 8 7 6 5 4 3 2 1

Printed in Heshan, Guangdong, China

This book was typeset in Esprit.
The illustrations were done in ink and watercolor on paper.

Candlewick Press
99 Dover Street
Somerville, Massachusetts 02144

visit us at www.candlewick.com

LITTLE FOX IN THE SNOW

Jonathan London   ILLUSTRATED BY Daniel Miyares

CANDLEWICK PRESS

Little foxling, little fox,
asleep in your hole,
in your halo of warmth—
it's time to wake up!

Your eyes open; your whiskers
twitch. You stretch,
then follow your breath . . .
out into the snow.

Little foxling, where will you go?

Hunger draws you
like a bow.
You must seek your target.
You must hunt!

What's that?
Your head tilts; your ears swivel.
Tiny footsteps
beneath the snow.

You pounce!

You crouch.

As sure as an arrow

you pierce the surface . . .

and pop up with a mouse!

Little fox, you cannot satisfy your hunger
with just a mouse.
More! your belly cries. *More!*

Little foxling, where will you go?

You flow like a shadow
across the fields.
You leave little paw prints
behind in the snow.

What's that?
White on white.

It sniffs.
You freeze.
You charge.
It flees.

Two shadows bound
across sun-sparkle snow.

A snowshoe hare is no match
for a fleet-footed fox.

Little foxling, belly full,
you make your way down
        to the snow-patched stream,
lap tiny tongue-curls of icy cold water.

Back up the bank,
by the trunk of a tree,
      you stop.
You sniff.
      What's that?
The scent of a she-fox,
a vixen!

Your heart
      quickens;
your ears stand tall.

But what do you see?
    Two eyes
in the shadows.

It sniffs.
        You freeze.

It charges!
You flee!

Little fox—you must *go go go!*
A fox is no match
for a wolverine.

You're a blur of fur
across the snow.
The sinking sun
sets your coat aglow.

Wolverine's eyes
            flare up
like struck matches —

but you follow your breath . . .

down into your hole.

Now curl up safe
(your breathing slows)
and go back to sleep
in your cozy burrow.

Little foxling, what do you dream?

*Of the bushy-tailed she-fox
leaping in the moonglow?*

Of your own little fox family
playing in the meadow?

Little foxling, little fox,
safe in your hole — tomorrow
you will go back
out into the snow.
But tonight, you can rest
in your halo of warmth.

Good night, little fox.